WILD CHILD

Forest's First Birthday Party

Tara Zann

[Imprint]
MAKE YOUR MARK

New York

[Imprint]
MAKE YOUR MARK

A part of Macmillan Publishing Group, LLC
175 Fifth Avenue, New York, NY 10010

WILD CHILD: FOREST'S FIRST BIRTHDAY PARTY. Copyright © 2017 by
Imprint. All rights reserved. Printed in the United States of
America by LSC Communications, Harrisonburg, Virginia.

Library of Congress Cataloging-in-Publication Data

Names: Zann, Tara, author. | Widdowson, Dan, illustrator.
Title: Wild child: Forest's first birthday party / Tara Zann ;
illustrations by Dan Widdowson.
Description: First edition. | New York : Imprint, 2017. | Series:
Wild child | Summary: Forest, who has grown up in the wild,
accompanies shy Olive to a classmate's birthday party,
where Olive hopes to make new friends and not embarrass
herself, and where, in spite of his popularity, Forest still
needs his best friend Olive to help him out.
Identifiers: LCCN 2017019962 (print) | LCCN 2016042885 (ebook) |
ISBN 9781250103901 (Ebook) | ISBN 9781250103895 (pbk.)
Subjects: | CYAC: Feral children—Fiction. | Birthdays—Fiction. |
Parties—Fiction. | Friendship—Fiction.
Classification: LCC PZ7.1.Z35 (print) | LCC PZ7.1.Z35 Wi 2017
(ebook) | DDC [Fic]—dc23
LC record available at https://lccn.loc.gov/2017019962

Our books may be purchased in bulk for promotional,
educational, or business use. Please contact your local
bookseller or the Macmillan Corporate and Premium Sales
Department at (800) 221-7945 ext. 5442 or by e-mail at
MacmillanSpecialMarkets@macmillan.com.

Book design by Ellen Duda
Illustrations by Dan Widdowson
Imprint logo designed by Amanda Spielman

First edition, 2017

1 3 5 7 9 10 8 6 4 2

mackids.com

If to you this book does not belong
put it back now; you don't have long.
For down on a piñata Forest will swing,
to take back this stolen thing!

For all kids and kids-at-heart,

especially J and Z—stay wild.

Chapter
1

Josie Letay's house stood in front of Olive and Forest like a big blue present waiting to be unwrapped. It especially looked like a present *today*, because today it was dressed up with shiny streamers and gold balloons for Josie's eighth birthday party.

Olive was dressed up, too: New overalls. New light-up sneakers. New Olive.

She had embarrassed herself at every one of Josie's parties so far, but this year, she was finally going to get it right.

Except they were already twenty-three minutes late.

Forest sprang out of the car, landing on all fours like a wild cat ready to party-pounce. Olive eagerly stepped out after him, and her dad honked the horn as they rushed to the door.

"HONK, HONK, HONK!" Forest yelled over his shoulder.

"HONK, HONK, Forest! Have fun! And Olive, remember your goal," her dad called.

"We'll have fun, Dad," she said. Olive knew that sometimes just saying things made them true. That's what a goal was: a wish that you said out loud.

I will have fun and make new friends, she thought.

I will not embarrass myself like last time or the time before, she thought.

I will be the bigger person and try to get along with Josie, she thought.

That last one was going to be hard, especially after the *Wizard of Oz* play. Josie had been the most popular girl in school since kindergarten, while Olive had been a loner—until Forest had literally dropped out of a redwood tree and into her life a few weeks ago. But Olive knew she could do anything with Forest by her side. Since he had come to live with her family, her shyness had disappeared.

Well, it had at least shrunk. Her stomach bopped like the balloons tied to

Josie's porch, all mixed up with excitement and nervousness.

Forest leaped onto the porch and rapped his knuckles against the wood, just like a woodpecker. Olive smoothed her hair down with one hand.

"Forest help Olive with hair." He ripped the sparkly purple bow off the present Olive was carrying and stuck it right on top of her head. She admired her reflection in the door's glass—Forest was developing a unique fashion sense.

"Thanks, Forest," she said.

Josie's mom opened the door. She looked a little frazzled already; the huge blond bun on top of her head was drooping to one side.

Olive gulped. Seeing Mrs. Letay

reminded her that at Josie's party last year, Olive slipped and fell into a bucket of water balloons. She broke every single one with her butt and had to spend the rest of the party in wet pants. Did Josie's mom remember the water balloon thing?

"Sorry we're late, Mrs. Letay," Olive said in a small voice. Her heart started to sputter.

"Josie's mom need help finding birds?" Forest said, pointing at Mrs. Letay's hair. "Nest on head empty."

Olive blushed. "Forest!"

"It's all right, Olive." Mrs. Letay sighed, adjusting her hair with both hands. "So *you're* Forest. Follow me, you two—the party's already in full swing."

Mrs. Letay led them down a long garden path. *Just a little hiccup*, Olive thought. *Maybe this* will *be fine. No, more than fine—good. Great. It will be—*

"Candy!" Forest cried, and dove for the ground.

Before Olive could stop him, he scooped up a handful of decorative glass pebbles from the landscaping and popped them into his mouth. Then he spit them out, and one flew across the yard and pinged against a bird feeder.

"Ow. Bad candy," he said, rubbing his cheek.

Mrs. Letay stopped and stared at the spit-covered stones scattered across her yard.

Olive piped up. "He's still confused about what's candy and what's not candy, Mrs. Letay. He won't try to eat anything else in your yard. Right, Forest?"

"Right, Olive." Forest held his jaw. Olive hoped his teeth were okay, because when they went to the dentist last week, Forest had climbed out the window and run all the way home.

Mrs. Letay smiled, but it was the kind of smile Olive gave her dad when she said his scrambled eggs were yummy—really, the eggs were cold and slimy, but she didn't want to make him feel bad. It was a *polite* smile.

They started walking again, but Olive's insides twisted up with a serious case of the Worries. Questions flooded her head: *Is Forest ready for a birthday party? Is getting a new start with Josie even possible?*

A few steps later, Mrs. Letay opened the gate to the backyard, and what they saw made Olive's Worries disappear.

Josie Letay's Amazing Birthday Party Extravaganza was just like she remembered, except better. The huge backyard was huger than before, the pool was a sparklier blue, and a bigger mountain of candy and snacks was spread across the picnic table in the center of everything. The yard was dotted with blue and purple balloons—Olive knew these were Josie's favorite colors—and streamers were woven in and out of the Letays' tall fence. In one corner, a magician in a pink suit was making balls disappear under cups. Josie's rabbit was outside in a pen. And from the looks of it, half the school was there.

Forest had a zillion questions—about

the magician, magic, the bunny, the streamers, the sprinkler, the swimming pool, and the magician again. He was especially confused about magic.

"Olive, what kind of tent is that?" Forest asked. He happened to be pointing smack in the middle of the yard, where a towering bounce house stood.

"It's not a tent, Forest. It's a bounce house!" Olive beamed. Perfect. That was the word for it. The party was perfect, and today Olive and Forest were going to be

perfect, too. "It's like when we jump on the bed, except the jumps are much higher, and Dad's not around to yell at us."

"Forest!" a bouncing girl yelled, her pigtails flapping up and down. "Look how high I can jump!"

Forest turned to Olive. His big brown eyes were even wider than usual and melting like chocolate ice cream. "Bounce house make you fly like bird? We go inside?"

"Yeah, but first we have to say hi to Josie. You know . . . start off on the right foot."

Forest lifted his left foot up like a flamingo. "Stay like this whole party?"

"No, Forest. It's an expression. It means we need to do things right." Forest

lowered his leg. "We also have to put her gift on the table."

Forest suddenly looked worried. "Forest didn't bring gift for Josie."

"It's okay, this gift is from both of—"

But before she could finish, Forest sped off, quick as a cheetah.

"Forest!" she called after him. Olive searched for him under the table and in the line of kids waiting for the bounce house, but she couldn't find him anywhere. She did find Josie talking and laughing with a group of their classmates right next to her mountain of presents.

Olive tugged at her braids. She really, really wished Forest was by her side—without Forest, all the courage she had built up suddenly popped like a birthday balloon.

But Olive took a deep breath and walked toward Birthday Present Mountain alone. Three steps closer, two steps closer, one step away . . .

"Hi Josie happy birthday!" she blurted out. Josie snapped her head toward Olive, her dark blond hair bouncing.

"Hi, Olive. Thanks for coming." Josie

smiled, but it was small and polite, just like her mom's smile had been earlier.

"Thanks for inviting us."

"Us? Did Forest come with you?" Josie asked. The polite smile turned into a real one.

"Yeah, but . . . I'm not sure where he is right now," Olive said.

Josie's face dropped. "Maybe later we can hang out when you find him?"

"Definitely," Olive said, feeling a sudden burst of confidence. Josie jogged over to her mom, who was waving at her to greet someone. "Maybe later" was Okay. Not Good. Definitely not Great.

"*Olive. Oooooooolive*," a voice hissed from above.

She looked up and gasped—Forest was dangling upside down from the tippy-top of one of the bounce house's towers.

Chapter
2

The tower swayed under Forest's weight. It shook and shuddered. His toes were slipping. . . .

The butterflies in Olive's stomach were like a flood—no, a stampede. Forest was going to fall right onto the table of presents.

Thankfully, Forest easily crawled down

the tower like a spider and ran toward Olive. Relief washed over her.

"Forest, you can't climb on everything like you do at home . . ." she started.

He pulled a fistful of bright yellow tulips from behind his back and wiggled them in Olive's face. "Present for Josie."

"Flowers?" Olive quickly scanned the yard and spotted the big hole Forest had made in the flower patch. Uh-oh.

"Flowers as present? No, Olive." Forest shook his head, as if giving flowers as a present was the craziest idea in the world. "Look."

Olive looked closer and saw the fat, pink worms curled in the dirt dangling from the flowers' roots. She took the little guys into her hands, and Forest threw the wormless flowers over his shoulder. . . . And they hit Mrs. Letay right in the face.

Olive burned red all the way down to her toes.

"Forest," Mrs. Letay said through gritted teeth. Olive quickly put the worms in her pocket while Mrs. Letay bent down to get the torn-up tulips. "Did you pull these up from my flower garden?"

Forest's face was getting red, too, like

it did when he realized he had done something wrong but didn't know what or why. Forest didn't know that grown-ups like to keep flowers in the ground, just to look at. Olive didn't really get it, either.

Okay—quick thinking.

"Mrs. Letay, Forest was just letting the flowers . . . breathe. We'll put them back now, good as new."

Mrs. Letay handed the tulips to Olive.

She was about to say something but caught sight of the dog trying to drink from the punch bowl again. "Rex!" she called, running away.

"Forest, there you are!" Josie screamed. She was getting into the bounce house. "Come bounce!"

"Bounce with me, Forest!" another partygoer cried.

"No, bounce with me!"

No one had noticed Forest until Josie did—but that was one of the things that was special about Josie. People caught her excitement for things like it was the flu.

Forest tugged Olive's arm, pulling her toward the bounce house, but Olive didn't budge. She needed to put the flowers back—fix things—before doing anything else. "Go ahead, Forest. I'll be there in a sec," Olive said.

Forest was giving her a case of the Worries. Big time. Maybe bouncing would keep him busy for a while. She could join Forest—and Josie—as soon as she put the tulips back.

Forest darted away again, climbed up the side of the bounce house, and rolled over the top, landing with a *plop* and a bounce. Josie squealed with happiness. Olive gently buried the tulips back in the dirt until they were good as new. Now she could work on making friends.

Yep. It was that easy. *I will go hang out with Josie.*

Olive brushed the dirt off her pants and walked right to the edge of the crowd of kids around the bounce house. There were a *lot* of them. She shouted, "Excuse me!" and "Can I get through?" until she practically lost her voice, but Forest didn't hear her. He kind-of-maybe saw her for a second, but then Josie pulled

him into a double-spin bounce and he disappeared.

Olive suddenly felt very, very small.

Someone tapped her shoulder. Turning, she saw a boy a whole head shorter than her whose jet-black hair pointed up like a shark fin.

"Excuse me your bow is crooked," he said in one breath.

"No, it's not." Olive reached up and touched the bow. It totally was. "It's supposed to be like that."

"Oh, okay." The boy adjusted his glasses. "Are you Olive? I've heard Forest talk about you. He's in one of my after-school groups. I'm in second grade." The boy said everything really fast, like the words were hot and burning his tongue.

"Yeah. I'm Olive."

"I'm Herbert." His shark-fin hair swayed side to side. "Colton calls me Herbot. Like robot? He says it like it's a bad thing, but it's really not."

Olive made a face. The syllables of Colton's name—COL. TON.—were like two annoying pokes in her ears. He was not very nice.

"Forest lives with you, right?" Herbert asked.

"Right." Olive had spent a lot of time trying to explain Forest to people. "We're best friends, but sometimes I call him my frother, because he's like my friend and my brother, and he calls me his frister because I'm like his friend and sister. There's not a good real word for it, so we made some up."

"Cool." Herbert stood there, not talking. *Did he run out of words because he was saying them so fast? Am I making friends? What should I do next?* Her brain was a spinning top. Before she could think of anything else, her hand shot up in the air.

"High five?" she said uncertainly.

Herbert immediately slapped her palm with his. His hand was sticky with something, but she didn't even wipe hers on her pants. Forest wouldn't be grossed out by sticky stuff, and neither would she.

They had high-fived the quietness away. Olive told him about the gymnastics class she and Forest took after school, and Herbert talked excitedly about knights, his favorite topic. Knights had squires. Knights went on quests. Knights had to eat bugs when they were traveling in the countryside.

Olive remembered the worms in her pocket. "I forgot about these guys." She plucked them out of her overalls and reached out her hand to show Herbert.

Except he wasn't interested. Instead he jumped, screamed, and fell backward onto the ground.

Oh, no! Olive crouched down, cupping the worms close to her chest. Herbert's eyes were wide with fear.

"Sorry, Herbert, I didn't know you were afraid of worms," she said.

"What?!" he said, his voice high. "I'm not!"

Yell-y voice. Big eyes. Crinkled forehead. All the things her brother, Ryan, did when he *insisted* he wasn't afraid of frogs. But when Forest brought a frog inside the house, Ryan had run away screaming.

"I won't get them in your face again, I promise."

Herbert uncrinkled his forehead and sat up as Olive unfurled her hands. The worms squirmed around in her palms. "My mom would say it's none of my business but . . . why do you have worms in your pocket?" he asked.

"This is Forest's gift to Josie. He likes to dig them up because it reminds him of living in the trees. Sometimes we play a game and figure out what letters they look like."

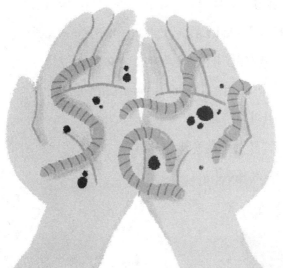

Herbert leaned forward and pointed. "This one kind of looks like the letter *S*."

Olive tilted her head. "That one does, too." She realized a lot of worms look like the letter *S*. She put them on the ground, and Herbert breathed a sigh of relief.

"Olive! Come fly!" Forest called. Olive and Herbert had to look way, way up to see him—he was jumping so high, he blotted out the sun. Kids clung to his arms like they were all monkeys in a barrel. And when Forest jumped, they jumped, too. He did a double jump. Then a double backflip. Then a triple backflip. His T-shirt billowed out like a parachute.

"Look!"

Bounce.

"Olive!"

Bounce. Bounce.

"Come!"

Bounce.

Finally, Forest could help her get in.

"Herbert, come on," Olive called. "Let's go bounce."

But Herbert stayed stuck in place. "Actually, the bounce house is kind of crazy right now and I get nervous around so many people so I'm just going to hang out here for a while," he said, digging his shoe into the dirt again. His shark fin drooped to one side, like it was sad, too.

Olive paused. She felt as though her body was a magnet being pulled in two directions. But she couldn't leave the only friend she had made at the party. And she also didn't want to.

"How about we play with Josie's bunny, instead?" Olive asked.

Herbert's face lit up. "I'm not scared of bunnies."

"Hey, Forest!" Olive yelled. "Herbert and I are going to pet the bunny!"

Forest yelled something back, but Olive and Herbert were already running to the bunny enclosure.

Chapter 3

There was a small sign on the pen that said, MY NAME IS MR. NIBBLES LETAY.

Olive and Herbert crouched over the black-and-white bunny to pet it. It shook under Olive's hand—but if she were a tiny ball of fluff at a person party, Olive would be scared, too.

"Hi, Mr. Nibbles," Olive said. Mr. Nibbles

quivered his nose at her. Then Herbert patted Mr. Nibbles and sneezed so hard, he fell backward onto his butt. Mr. Nibbles darted under Olive to hide.

"Gesundheit," Olive said. "My favorite way to say 'bless you.' "

"Thanks." Herbert wiped his nose on his sleeve. "I'm allergic to cats. I guess I'm allergic to *conejitos*, too."

The word exploded in her ear like

fireworks. She wanted to know what it meant. Immediately.

"What are . . . co-neh-hee-toes?" Olive asked.

"That's Spanish for 'bunny.'" Herbert took a bright blue bandanna out of his pocket and wiped his nose. "My brother teaches me."

"That's cool," Olive said. She wanted to learn as many new words as she could. "How do you say 'cool'?"

"*Chévere*," Herbert said.

"How do you say 'awesome'?"

"*Genial. Increíble. Estupendo.*"

"*Estupendo*?" Olive asked. "That sounds mean, kind of sounds like 'stupid.'" Her brother called her that once and she didn't like the way it felt.

"Stupid is *estúpido*, which also sounds like stupid. But there's *bobo*, too," he whispered, like he was afraid someone was going to hear him say it, "which is nicer but not that nice because it means 'dum-dum.'"

At Olive's insistence, Herbert started to teach her nicer words—*dormilona* (sleepyhead), *gansa* (silly goose), *pingüino* (penguin)—because they were classic nicknames her dad used, and she pretended she didn't like them even though she secretly did. All the while, they made a little bunny-sized obstacle course for Mr. Nibbles—the first Bunny Olympics.

They were trying to get Mr. Nibbles to jump through a hoop (Olive's necklace) when Olive heard a low rumbling noise and a bunch of loud voices coming from the bounce house. Even Mr. Nibbles sprang up on his back legs and perked up his ears to check out the noise. Kids were sliding out of the bounce house like popcorn overflowing a bag, and everyone was yelling for Forest to come out, too—he finally popped through the bounce-house flaps, his massive hair fuzzy and full of static.

"Forest is king of the bounce house!" Josie yelled.

Everyone started to chant as they lifted Forest onto their shoulders. "All hail, King Forest! All hail, King Forest!"

The parents kept telling everyone to quiet down, but eventually they gave up and started chanting, "KING FOREST! KING FOREST!" too, even a dad who got

smacked in the face by someone's smelly shoe. Only Mrs. Letay looked nervous— she kept holding her hands up like she was ready to catch Forest at any second.

Forest crawled over everyone like a squirrel, squishing people with his bare feet. He plucked party hats off every- one's heads, the strings snapping with little *pop*s, and looped the elastic bands behind his ears until every single hat was stacked on his chin. It looked like he had a huge, pointy beard.

Forest leaped on top of the picnic table, dodging and dancing around the ocean of hands that were trying to get his attention. He tossed pretzels, gummies, and cheese puffs to the kids one by one and yelled, "Fetch!"

"Hey, Forest!" Olive called, waving to him. "Come over here!"

"Olive!" Forest broke into a huge grin, though it was hard to see with his party-hat beard. He scooped candy from a bowl on the table and threw it, hard and far, into the grass. While everyone was distracted scrambling for it, Forest jumped off the table and ran toward Olive.

"Forest will love this," Olive said to Herbert. "I bet he can train Mr. Nibbles."

Forest leaped over the bunny enclosure's tiny white fence and wrapped Olive
into a hug. "Party is hard, Olive."
Mr. Nibbles hopped up to Forest, who
bent down and shook his small bunny
paw. "Hello, Mr. Nibbles."

Olive and Herbert explained Bunny
Olympics to Forest, who built a seesaw
from one of his party hats and a flat piece

of tree bark they found on the ground. Olive and Herbert cheered as Forest coached Mr. Nibbles back and forth over the seesaw. Then the bunny started to hop around and wiggle his butt.

"I think Mr. Nibbles needs *el baño*," Herbert said.

"*¿Me encanta el baño?*" Forest replied.

Herbert cracked like an egg. He rolled with laughter, repeating, "Forest loves the bathroom!" over and over. Mr. Nibbles got excited and climbed onto Herbert's chest, which made him sneeze like crazy.

"Forest speak better animal than Spanish. Learn from tourists in park, but only a little," Forest said.

"What's Mr. Nibbles saying?" Olive piped up between her own giggles.

Forest crouched low and Mr. Nibbles sniffed the hats still perched on his chin. Forest cupped his ear next to Mr. Nibbles, listening.

"Mr. Nibbles want to *run*," Forest said. Then he picked up Mr. Nibbles and plopped him on the other side of the pen.

"Forest, no!" Olive's heart thudded in her chest. She shot up and started to chase Mr. Nibbles, who was now bounding across the yard.

Josie's bunny. Escaping. Josie would never be friends with Olive if that happened.

The other kids started to run alongside Olive, too, hot on Mr. Nibbles's fuzzy tail, which only made Mr. Nibbles run

faster. Herbert jogged a wide circle and jumped in front of the speeding bunny, but Mr. Nibbles flew through his legs. Olive dove through Herbert's legs, too, sliding her body over the grass and dirt, before Herbert toppled over, sneezing. She barely touched Mr. Nibbles's fluffy butt before he slipped away again.

Breathing heavily, side aching, Olive looked up to see that Mr. Nibbles was making a beeline for the magician's table—straight for a hole in Josie's fence. Her whole body felt heavy and slow. She'd never get there in time.

Just then, Forest swung from a branch and landed on all fours in front of Mr. Nibbles. The bunny jumped right into his arms.

Olive ran over. Thank goodness, Mr. Nibbles seemed okay, even though his nose was quivering a million quivers a second. Now they could put him back in his enclosure and everything would be—

"And for my last and best trick!" the magician in the pink pinstriped pants cried, "I will make this bunny disappear!"

Forest tilted his head in confusion when the magician plucked Mr. Nibbles out of his grasp and covered the bunny with a colorful scarf. Then, with a flourish, the magician pulled the scarf away. Mr. Nibbles was nowhere to be seen. The kids cheered.

Forest roared at the top of his lungs.

Chapter 4

"WHERE MR. NIBBLES?!" Forest yelled.

Forest was in his lion pose—hair puffed out like a mane, hands up around his face. The pointy hats on his chin looked even pointier.

And everyone stared like Forest was an animal in the zoo. Olive needed some more quick thinking.

"It's okay, Forest," Olive said. She

looked at the magician. "Can you make Mr. Nibbles come back now? Please?"

The magician eagerly waved the scarf over his palm. When he took it away, Mr. Nibbles was sitting there on his hind legs. Everyone clapped, except Forest, who gently grabbed Mr. Nibbles and walked away grumbling to himself. Olive followed him and watched as he took a handful of streamers from the fence,

made a bunny-sized pouch, and strapped Mr. Nibbles to his back.

"Bunny safe with Forest," he said. "No more disappear."

A shadow fell over them. It was Josie, and her arms were filled with a rainbow of water balloons.

"Uh, Forest?" Josie said, the balloons jiggling. "I brought water balloons for us to play with."

Josie looked at Olive, then down at the water balloons, like she was remembering when Olive broke them all last year. Olive covered her butt with her hands to make it clear that she didn't plan on sitting on them this time.

Forest tilted his head at the balloons.

"Water baboons?" He made baboon noises.

"No, silly!" Josie said. "Water ballllll-looooooooons."

Forest poked a small hole in a balloon with his massive cone beard. A tiny jet of water shot out, which Forest aimed right into Mr. Nibbles's mouth.

"Mr. Nibbles thirsty. Olive want some? Look sweaty."

Olive blushed. She was sweaty only because she was chasing Mr. Nibbles around the whole yard. Because of Forest.

"I want to try, too!" Josie poked a hole in another balloon with Forest's beard. "Here, Olive," she said. Instead of squirting water in Olive's mouth, she sprayed some on Olive's shoes. "Oops. Sorry!"

Olive tried not to scowl. "I'm sure it was an accident."

"Let's do the water balloon toss!" Josie said. She called everyone over and started to hand out water balloons. "Hey, Olive? Is it okay if I'm partners with Forest?" she whispered.

Oh. She wanted to say *no*, but Josie actually sounded . . . nice. Like she really wanted to be partners with Forest. Olive couldn't say no. Well, she *could*, but that's not what maybe-friends did. Josie smiled at Olive, waiting . . .

"Sure, Josie. I can be his partner another time."

"I'm sure you can find another partner. Thanks!" Josie chirped, and ran to Forest.

Herbert walked over. "Want to be partners? No pressure. My dad says you should never rush people when they're making a decision."

"My dad usually just runs around trying to remember where he put stuff."

Mrs. Letay frantically lined up partners across from each other into two neat, straight rows in the middle of the yard. Herbert stood across from Olive at one end.

Olive scanned the row for Forest, and finally spotted him—and what she saw made the Worries rear up again. Forest's eyes were wide, and his head snapped back and forth between the water balloons.

He crouched low.

Uh-oh. Olive's stomach dropped. That was Forest's battle position. He thought that they were going to attack each other.

Forest cried out, breaking from his side of the line, and grabbed the empty balloon bucket away from Mrs. Letay, which he put on his head like a helmet. He ran through the middle of every-one, madly spearing water balloons with his pointy hat beard. One kid burst

into tears when Forest popped his balloon, but Forest kept running and poking and popping.

Olive had to stop him before it was a total disaster. She sprinted toward him.

"Time out, time out, time out!" she yelled. A water balloon clonked her on the head and bounced off her ear, but she didn't stop running toward Forest. Herbert followed after her, whistling like mad. "Uh, Forest wants to change the game to . . . Monkey in the Middle!" she yelled.

Josie shrieked with delight and tossed her water balloon over Forest's head. He threw the bucket helmet off his head, launched himself in the air, angled his chin up, and speared the water balloon easily. It burst open with a watery *sploop*.

The other kids joined in, too, and soon they were all tossing water balloons over Forest, who lunged at every single one of them until his hat beard was smashed to a pile of soggy mush.

"Mrs. Letay looks like she's about to burst," Herbert said.

With a whoosh, Forest leaped to the fence and frantically tried to crawl under a bunch of streamers. Mr. Nibbles helped by clawing at the streamers, too. Olive watched in horror as Forest started tearing them all down trying to burrow like an animal . . .

"Forest . . . what are you doing?" Josie said. For the first time all day, Josie looked less than happy.

"This is a game we play at home," Olive said quickly.

"Another game?" Josie asked uncertainly.

"Yeah! Wrapping up like a mummy?" Olive said, pointing at the streamers. "It's so fun! We do it all the time."

"Forest cocoon," he whispered.

Olive could see only his eyes. Her stomach felt like she had swallowed Forest's whole worm collection—she realized that Forest didn't like being a cocoon. Not at all.

She started to pull the streamer cocoon apart to get him out, but the streamers were too tight and he was wiggling too much.

Rrrrrrrrrr1P! Forest stuck two arms through his streamer cocoon and hopped around the yard, arms flailing, like a baby bird. When Forest finally emerged, his hair looked like a tornado standing still.

"Forest! Are you oka—"

Interrupting her was the blare of a huge horn right in Olive's ear!

"PIÑATA!" someone screamed.

Chapter 5

"Ow," Olive said, rubbing her ear, which was ringing from the loud sound. It was louder than Herbert's whistle. She turned, still massaging her ear with one hand.

Josie was standing right behind her with a silver bicycle horn in her hand.

"Forest, come on!" Josie yelled, blaring the horn a few more times in the air.

"Wow, look at that," Herbert said, craning his neck up. Olive saw it, too: a big piñata in the shape of a donkey hanging from the branches. It was the biggest piñata Olive had ever seen.

"What happen to donkey?" Forest asked, pulling off the last of the streamers.

"We have to line up first, then you'll

see," Josie replied. "Other than presents, this is the *best* part of the party!"

Mrs. Letay lined everyone up from youngest to oldest, putting Olive and Herbert first in line. "You can go first, Olive. I don't think you'll do too much damage." She looked at Forest, and her face twisted into a frown. "Forest . . . I have a feeling you're a different story.

Back of the line, dear."

Forest scratched his head in confusion. "I thought we no keep donkey in backyard?"

Everyone watched as Mrs. Letay lowered the piñata, listening for the candy moving inside. She put the silky blind-fold around Olive's head and spun her around and around and around, until Olive was teetering. Steadying herself, Olive gripped the plastic bat tightly and reached out and up, up, up until . . .

Tap. Now that she knew where the piñata was, Olive pulled the bat over her shoulder like she was in the batting cages with her dad. Her face exploded into a grin. Being first was a lot of pressure, but she wanted to show everyone that she was little and quiet but also strong. She pulled the bat waaaaaay back, and . . .

SMACK.

The air around Olive exploded with noise: a *smack*, *crack*, and *whoosh* as the piñata sailed away from her. Did she break it? Olive felt the wind of the piñata on her face . . .

CLUNK. The piñata banged into her. "Ow," she said, rubbing her shoulder. She had hit it so hard, it swung back at her. Before she could raise the bat again, she heard a familiar rush of feet next to her.

"Uh-oh," Herbert said.

"DONKEY NO HIT OLIVE!" Forest yelled.

"Forest?" Olive called out.

But it was too late. Olive pulled up her blindfold just in time to see Forest jump up and wrap himself around the piñata like a sloth around a tree branch. Mr. Nibbles's ears flopped in the wind as the piñata and Forest swung wildly back and forth. Kids shrieked with laughter.

Then, the rope snapped. Olive gasped. Forest fell to the ground, landing on his feet with the piñata tucked under his arm. The giggling, screaming kids crowded around him.

Olive could hardly breathe now. She was worried about Forest, but she was also worried about the party. If Forest wrecked the piñata, no one else would have the chance to hit it. She nudged herself between two kids to where Forest had landed. . . . Forest was jumping back and forth, clutching the piñata tightly.

Olive's quick-thinking tank was almost on empty. But she had one more idea left.

She could save the party and *not* embarrass herself.

"CAPTURE THE PIÑATA!" she screamed, throwing her hands up in the air.

Everyone sprinted after Forest, who took off running. Olive knew it was impossible to catch him—he was faster than everything in the world. His legs were moving so fast, it didn't even look like his feet were hitting the ground.

Plus, the backyard was *huge*. It seemed bigger than a football field.

"Olive, jump!" Josie jumped over a huge rock. A few feet ahead of them, Forest launched himself over a stump and disappeared behind a bush. Olive and Josie paused, panting.

"*AIIIIIIIEEEEAA!*" Forest jumped out of a tree. He sailed right over their heads and landed on the donkey piñata like he was a knight on his steed, skidding on the grass between them. Chocolate was smeared across his face and streamers sailed behind him like a flag. Laughing

kids followed him around the yard like a school of fish. Olive lost Josie in the crowd.

Olive felt something tickling her shoulders and realized her braids had come loose from all the running. Her fingers rushed to rebraid them—she couldn't go walking around looking like this.

Her breath caught up with her. Chasing Forest was exhausting.

Making new friends and trying not to embarrass herself was exhausting.

Herbert jogged up next to her, then collapsed on the ground with his tongue out, breathing heavily. "Forest is so fast!" he said.

And maybe she was so busy trying to

look after Forest, she was ignoring the friend she had just made.

Olive finished braiding her hair. It was a bit messy, but Forest didn't care about what everyone else thought. He didn't think about having fun. He just *had* fun.

He had the right idea. And so did she.

"Herbert, there's no one in the bounce house right now. Want to go? We'll have so much room."

"Sure. First one there wins?" Herbert asked Olive.

Olive was panting again by the time they reached the bounce house. Herbert won, but only by a teensy bit. She wondered if the shark-fin hairstyle made him faster.

"Good race, Olive. But I think I'm done

running forever. I'm into bouncing only from now on."

Herbert and Olive took turns launching each other up into the air like rockets and jumped around until they were dizzy and Olive's legs felt wobbly as Jell-O. She plopped down on the sticky plastic to rest while Herbert told Olive all about how knights never took baths. Olive's verdict about knights: smelly, but interesting.

Out of the corner of her eye, she saw the huge swarm of kids running toward the bounce house. They were still screaming, chasing . . . and not stopping. Suddenly, they rushed around the bounce house like a raging river. Olive thought she heard a faint *rrrrip.*

"Uh-oh." Herbert stopped bouncing. "Did I rip my pants again?"

Olive was about to say no when she felt something under her: a slow kind of sinking, like the bounce house was melting. She put her ear against the wall . . . and eventually, even through all the noise from the piñata chase, heard something hissing.

Olive looked up. Herbert did, too.

The towers were drooping toward them. The walls were getting closer.

They were sinking. Sloooooowly.

Then fast.

Then faster.

Olive grabbed Herbert's hand.

"Herbert . . . I don't think it was your pants. The bounce house is deflating!"

They slid through the bounce house flaps and landed with a thud on the cool green grass. Everyone was yelling and scattering. Olive looked up just in time to see the entire structure collapse to the ground.

"Yikes." Herbert whistled under his breath.

Olive backed away in horror. There's no *way* any amount of quick thinking would fix this mess.

Mrs. Letay stood still as a statue, staring at the deflated bounce house with her mouth flopped open. "I'll find some duct tape . . ." she finally said, and walked off into the house.

Someone must have accidentally punctured it while they chased Forest. Olive's stomach twisted, as if someone was making it into a balloon animal. This was her fault—she had started the piñata chase. She needed to find Forest, so he could help fix everything: the piñata, the bounce house, the party before it fell apart. She just wanted everything to go back to normal.

Olive searched for the mass of kids chasing Forest so she could talk to him—but she quickly realized that no one was chasing him anymore. They were looking for him, because Forest was nowhere in sight.

Chapter 6

Olive caught up to Josie, who looked worried.

"I can't find Forest anywhere," she said.

"Forest is really good at hiding. He's probably in a tree," Olive said.

"Really?" Josie's eyes got wide.

"For sure. I'll help find him."

"Okay," Josie chirped. "Also, I really like your hair like that. It looks like Forest's."

"Thanks! Yours always looks great." Even though she was worried about Forest, Olive felt a small thrill of excitement. She and Josie had been getting along the whole day because of Olive's quick thinking. Maybe they could be better than okay—maybe they could actually be friends.

They split up, and Olive jogged over to the tree at the far side of Josie's yard. She hugged herself against the tree trunk and looked toward the sky, scouring the tree branches for any sign of Forest. But all she saw was a few squirrels chasing one another.

She stepped back. Something crunched and snapped and exploded

under her foot. Olive looked down—there was a piece of pink, squishy candy stuck to the bottom of her shoe.

"What the . . ." Olive searched the ground and spotted a trail of candy in the grass. She followed the trail, collecting fallen candy all the way to the side of the house, until she found the crushed piñata smashed next to a garden gnome. She frantically stuffed the candy back into the donkey's head while trying to push out the dents in the cardboard. But where was Forest?

Olive searched the yard with her eyes. She saw that Mrs. Letay had patched the hole in the bounce house with tape, though it was still a little saggy. Olive

heard someone sneeze and looked over to see Herbert a little ways away, wiping his nose with his bandanna again.

Herbert's nose gave Olive the greatest quick thinking of the day. Possibly the whole century.

Herbert and his allergies were going to find Forest.

Olive grabbed Herbert and started to walk around with Herbert's nose stretched way out.

"Okay, sniff reeaaaaaaaally deeply, Herbert," Olive coached. When they walked by a gnarled tree in the corner of Josie's yard, he started sneezing like crazy—especially when he got close to a big hole in the trunk.

Sure enough, there were tufts of

hair—and a whole lot of Forest—sticking out of the hole.

"Olive!" he cried. Forest jumped out and tackled her with a hug. Mr. Nibbles peeked out of his hair.

"Forest!" Olive waved the piñata in front of his face. "Quick, you have to help me fix this before Josie notices. . . ."

He backed away from her, and Olive saw his lip trembling. "Olive no listen," he said.

Before Olive could answer, Josie came tearing around the tree. "You found him!" She ran up to Forest, took his hand, and pulled him toward the house. "Forest, I need to show you something, and it's *very* important. . . ."

Josie tugged Forest back toward the

party. Josie didn't seem to care at all that Forest had destroyed her piñata. It was like she had forgotten about it altogether.

Olive slumped. Didn't Josie want her party to be perfect? Olive just didn't get it—she was trying so hard, and nothing made sense.

Then Olive saw what Josie was excited about: Mrs. Letay stood in the middle of the yard, holding a giant white and purple cake shaped like a castle. And it had eight huge glowing candles on top.

"Wow," Olive breathed. It was the best cake she had ever seen.

And Forest was running right for it.

"FIIIIIIIIIIIIIIIRE!" he screamed, waving his hands above his head.

Oh, no. Olive hadn't told Forest about birthday cakes. Or birthday candles. The thought hit her like the world's biggest water balloon. Josie might have been okay with Forest ruining the piñata and the bounce house and basically bunny-napping Mr. Nibbles, but there's no *way* she would think Forest ruining her cake was funny.

Olive took off.

She chased after Forest, her bare feet thudding against the ground. He had already sprinted past Josie, who stood there with a stunned look on her face. Forest was almost to Mrs. Letay, but maybe Olive was fast enough to catch him. She saw him grab the bowl of punch from the picnic table, some of the liquid splashing over the sides . . .

"Forest, what are you doing!" Olive cried, skidding to a halt between him and the tower of cake in Mrs. Letay's arms.

It was too late—but instead of dousing the cake, Forest poured the bowl of punch all over Olive.

Chapter 7

Everything—the bright red punch, the glittering ice cubes, the splash of cold—seemed like it was moving in slow motion. Other than Olive's own heart beating, everything was silent . . . until someone's giggle hit her like a wet snowball.

Olive wrapped her arms around herself, but it didn't help. Maybe her sopping-wet curls would hide her face.

Maybe she could go back to Forest's tree in the park and stay there forever.

"Oh, dear." Mrs. Letay set the cake on the picnic table and gently helped Olive sit on the bench. "I'll get you a towel, honey."

A piece of ice fell out of Olive's hair and plinked onto the picnic table. Cold punch dripped down her arms. Olive met

Forest's eyes: They were big, wet, sad, and more than a little confused.

"Olive don't want Forest to put out fire?" he asked quietly.

Olive couldn't even speak—she just shook her head no. She felt shy all over again. Old Olive.

Josie looked at Olive, and Olive saw the flash of an idea in her eyes. "How about we sing 'Happy Birthday' now? Go!" Josie said.

Everyone sang "Happy Birthday" (everyone except Olive), and Josie took a deep breath in and blew out her candles in one puff. Olive's body loosened up with some relief—now Josie was doing the quick thinking. Everyone clapped,

and smoke from the candles floated up over the cake like a dirty gray cloud.

At least everyone would be distracted with sugary cake. Olive hoped Josie's mom would bring back a towel big enough to crawl under and hide until her dad came and picked them up. Josie gave the first way-too-big piece of cake to Olive—and it even had a big purple rose made of frosting on it. A special corner slice. Olive smiled at her, and Josie smiled back.

Herbert scooted onto the bench next to her. There was frosting on his nose and glasses. "Hey, Olive. You smell like the candy aisle in the grocery store."

Olive sniffed her hair. Herbert was right—she smelled like Wildberry Fruit Punch. "Thanks, Herbert."

"You're welcome. I think Forest is trying to get your attention. Should he have a hose?"

Olive looked up to see Forest waving one hand in the air and dragging the hose across the lawn with the other. She didn't think this day could get worse, but . . .

Forest angled the hose above his head and took his thumb off the nozzle, dousing himself in water. He let it run down his whole body until his clothes were heavy and dripping. After he was completely soaked, he let go of the hose, which wriggled all over the lawn, spewing

water. Kids held on to their cake while they sprang out of the hose's path.

Now Forest was sopping wet, even more than she was, and she felt so much less alone.

A bubble of shyness popped in Olive, and she laughed. And everyone started laughing with her, including Forest.

"What Olive want to do?" Forest said, his voice booming across the yard.

Olive hopped down from her bench and landed on the ground. Mud shot up from under her shoes—the ground was soaked from Forest's hose attack—and splatted right onto Josie's new dress.

Oh, no. Oh, no, no, no, no, no.

"OLIVE SAY MUD FIGHT!" Forest bellowed.

Forest reached down, picked up a giant fistful of mud, and smacked it all right into his face.

Josie beamed. "Great idea, Olive!" she yelled, picking up mud with both her hands. She gave one handful to Olive.

"Thanks, Josie," Olive squeaked.

"You're welcome," Josie said. And then she splattered mud on her face, too.

Chapter 8

Kids shot around the yard, flinging mud at one another. No one was trying to dodge the mud bombs except the grown-ups, who scrambled to shield themselves.

Olive, though, stayed put in the towel Mrs. Letay had given her. Forest had distracted everyone, but she *felt* a little like a deflated bounce house. Something was wrong. The party was almost over, but she still had the Worries . . .

Forest, dripping wet with red-brown, icky, sticky mud goop, plopped down next to Olive on the bench. His butt squished on the wood.

"Olive—Forest sorry."

Forest's eyes looked watery, and also kind of muddy. Olive wiggled in her seat. She wanted to be mad at Forest for spilling punch all over her . . . but she just couldn't.

He scratched his head like he was thinking really hard or coming up with a plan. "*I'm* sorry. Is that right?" he asked, leaning forward eagerly. "Olive taught Forest to apple guys—"

Olive smiled. "Apologize."

"I'm sorry, Olive." Forest patted her on the back, leaving a big muddy handprint on her shirt. "But . . . why you no explain anything about bird day parties? Forest spent all day confused, like when Dad try to cook." He looked down at his mud-covered feet. "Olive did not help."

"But, Forest . . . I—I was trying to make sure the party went just right."

Forest shook his head wildly, flinging specks of muddy water all over the place.

"Forest always need Olive! Forest—I," he said, correcting himself, "want to be more like Olive always. Olive know rules for everything. And . . . Forest need help."

Olive's stomach tied up like a shoelace. She thought about everything—the Mr. Nibbles incident, the bounce house fiasco, the piñata debacle. Forest had needed her help all day, and Olive was too focused on herself to notice.

"Forest, I'm sorry, too. You're just so good at making friends. I wanted to be more like you today."

Forest's mouth dropped open. "Really, Olive?"

"Really," Olive said.

He lowered his voice to a whisper. "I tell you a secret?"

"Of course," Olive said, nodding.

"I miss my redwood home sometimes. Olive's world too big and scary for me."

Olive leaned her punch-drenched head on his shoulder. "It's big and scary for me, too. But I know we'll be okay, especially if we stick together. Can I tell *you* a secret now?" Olive asked.

"Of horse," Forest said.

"Olive missed Forest today, too."

She hugged him, and the Worries disappeared. Forest beamed, his teeth

shining white against all the brownish mud. "Forest made one wish on fire sticks," he said.

"You're not supposed to tell—" Olive started.

"Forest wish Olive no mad at Forest. Forest wish Olive his best friend. Forest wish Olive have the best bird day party in the whole world!"

Laughing, Olive twisted some punch out of her hair. "That's three wishes, Forest. And you totally don't have to wish I'm your best friend—'cause I *am* your best friend. But just because we are best friends doesn't mean we're *only* friends with each other."

"Shake on it?" Forest asked, a very serious expression on his face.

Olive held out her hand. But Forest stood up and started shaking his body like a wet dog until Olive started doing it, too.

"Best bird day!" Forest yelled, hopping and twirling around.

"It's 'birthday,' Forest. 'Birth. Day.'"

Forest's eyes became as wide as two pieces of cake. "You mean . . . no bird day party for Josie? Forest need to fix something—"

Behind them, Mrs. Letay shrieked. Olive whipped her head around to see that Josie's mom was running away from a bunch of squawking birds that were whirling and darting around her head like a feathery storm. They had exploded out of one of Josie's birthday presents.

"Too late!" Forest said. "Now it also bird day party. Forest was worried worms not enough for Josie."

Olive had to cover her mouth with her hand to keep from laughing. "Forest, I know you can't always be *in* the forest. But you're the best at bringing the forest to you. To us. And you know who else is good at bringing the forest to you?" Olive asked.

"Um . . ." Forest started looking around. "Herbert?"

"No!" Olive said, scooping up a huge handful of mud. "ME!!"

Olive flung the squishy mud into Forest's hair.

"MUD PARTY!" Forest and Olive yelled together. Then, with armfuls of mud, they ran into the fighting, muddy crowd of kids.

***

Olive couldn't see Mrs. Letay over the huge pile of rainbow laundry in her arms. Almost every kid was rolled up in a warm towel, exhausted from the mud fight. Forest and Olive and Herbert sat right on the ground, eating cake sprinkled with broken pieces of candy. The sun dried up the mud on their skin.

"So, Forest, the *coolest* thing is that you had to train fourteen *years* before becoming a knight!"

Even though Forest was fidgeting, he was doing a great job listening. He had been still for almost a whole minute, which was a new record for him— Olive was counting the seconds when she felt a *tap tap tap* on her shoulder. She turned around and looked up, squinting in the sun to see . . . Josie.

"Hi, Olive!" Josie's normally perfect hair was sopping wet and encrusted with mud. "I just wanted to say thank you for making my party so fun. It wouldn't have been the same without you."

"Wow, really?" Olive asked. "I mean . . . your birthday parties are always so perfect. I kind of worried we messed things up for you."

Josie laughed and pulled some cake out of her hair. "Are you KIDDING? All my other parties were perfect. But all my other parties were also sooooooooooo boring."

Olive blushed and shifted in her seat. "I was worried I was going to embarrass myself again."

"You totally did! But I've decided that embarrassing yourself is fun. See?" Josie said, gesturing to her filthy party dress. "Look how much fun I'm having!"

Olive's face hurt from smiling. She, Herbert, Forest, and *everyone* else started grabbing punch, water, and mud, laughing as they poured it onto their heads and one another.

"This best bird day party ever!" Josie yelled.

"This best friend ever!" Forest yelled, squeezing Olive's shoulders.

Olive happily dumped another cup of punch on her head. She couldn't agree more.

About the Author

Tara Zann can't imagine living in a place without tall trees. Just like Forest, she has a spirit of adventure, though she might use a zip line instead of swinging from tree to tree on a long, dangling vine. She has no official pets, but dozens of creatures tend to stop by her backyard tree house on a regular basis.

Read ALL the books in the WILD CHILD series!

Read on for a sneak peek at Forest's First Bully!

Read on for a sneak peek at Forest's First Bully!

Puffy, white marshmallow clouds hung in the sky outside of Olive Regle's classroom window, while a lawn mower buzzed across the football field with the insistence of a bee. Inside the classroom, Olive could almost smell the mown grass—the smell of summer vacation. The clock ticked and tocked, steady as a drum.

Josie Letay was giving her Summer Plans presentation. For vacation, she was going to a tropical island, then to a snow-capped mountain, then to an active volcano. Olive's legs jiggled anxiously in her seat—because in about sixty seconds, she would have to stand in front of the class, too.

Forest rocked back and forth with excitement at the desk next to her, his hair swaying with the movement of his body. Hearing Josie talk about traveling was practically making him drool; after

living his whole life in the trees, Forest wanted to see *everything*.

Olive's dad hadn't planned a trip (it was hard, since he had to work all the time), so Olive had written a speech about what she and Forest were going to do this summer. She had even typed up the speech on her dad's computer to help her memorize it and put the title in all capital letters because capital letters are Special and Important.

"Olive be okay," Forest whispered to her. He always knew when she was nervous. "You been saying speech while you sleep."

"I have?" Olive whispered back.

"Forest heard from bedroom nest." Forest had his own bed, but he preferred to sleep on a pile of shirts, pants, and dirty socks on top of Olive's bookshelf, next to her bed. It reminded him of the cozy tree nook he had slept in at Redwood National Park, where Olive first met him. Thankfully, though, there were no chipmunks or squirrels or bugs in his new nest. At least, not that Olive knew of. . . .

Olive leaned way over. "Do you think I'll mess up?"

"Not by a long snot," Forest replied.

Her face lit up like a lightbulb. She didn't even bother to correct him.

"And when we go to the Tornado Twister amusement park, the whole class is invited!" Josie said, finishing her speech with a flourish.

Whoops and cheers filled the room. Eric Keizer got so excited that he threw his pencil up, and with a *thwack*, it stuck in the ceiling. Some kids raised their hands in the air, like they were already riding the Tornado Twister. Forest, though, looked alarmed, most likely because he had no idea what an amusement park was, or that "tornado twister" was the name of an awesome roller coaster and not a natural disaster.

"Olive, I think you're next," said Mrs. Finn.

Olive nodded and walked to the front of the room, her hands trembling as she turned to face the class. Battling her shyness had gotten easier since she'd met Forest—she had even starred in the school play earlier this year—but speaking in front of people was still capital *H* Hard. When she cleared her throat, the noise came out more like a squeak.

Just when she finally felt ready to talk, her heart flapping like a crazed bird inside her chest, the door opened with a shriek and a bang. A tall, freckled shape appeared in the doorway.

Colton.

Late again. He was always disrupting Something Important.

It didn't help that Colton was a bully.